# To Mathilde

Originally published as *On puppy's nose, a grasshopper . . .* by Nefeli in Greece, October 2017

Text copyright © 2021 Rodoula Pappa
Illustration copyright © 2021 Seng Soun Ratanavanh

Book design by Melissa Nelson Greenberg

Library of Congress Cataloging-in-Publication Data available.
ISBN: 978-1-951836-14-6

Printed in China

10 9 8 7 6 5 4 3 2

CAMERON KIDS is an imprint of CAMERON + COMPANY

**CAMERON + COMPANY**
Petaluma, California
www.cameronbooks.com

# Beautiful Day!

Petite Poems for All Seasons

words by Rodoula Pappu

art by Seng Soun Ratanavanh

cameron kids

SPRING

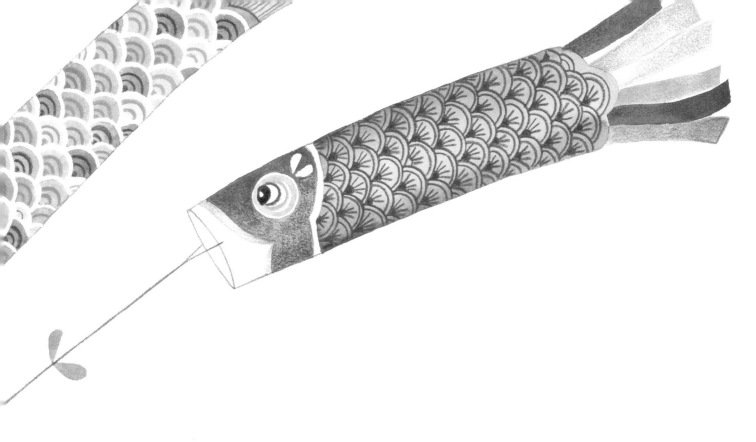

Look: in the sky
they blossomed again,
the kites!

Beautiful day!
Teach me, too, how to fly,
mother swallow.

On tender wings,
wide-open eyes—
butterfly.

I promise,
dewy little strawberry,
I won't pick you.

For the little lamb,
a new discovery—
a daisy!

SUMMER

What a deep sleep!
On puppy's nose,
a grasshopper.

On the pine tree,
a whole orchestra—
dz dz dz . . .

So shy,
such red cheeks,
little peach!

Among the reeds,
a new galaxy—
fireflies.

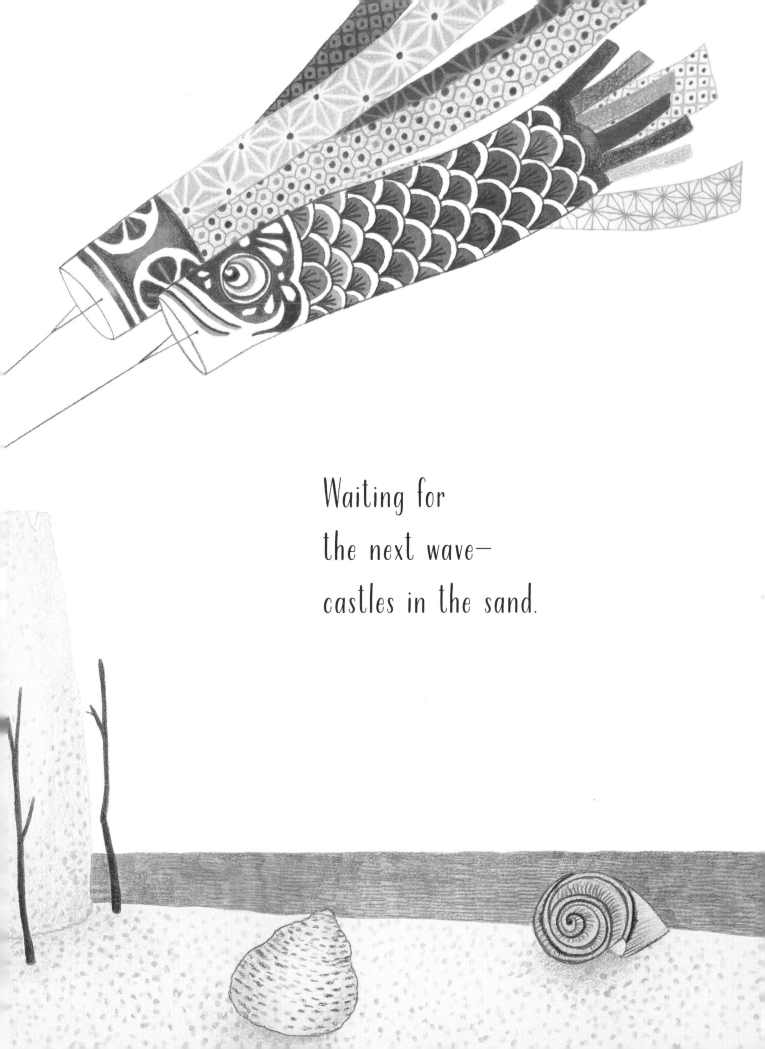

Waiting for
the next wave—
castles in the sand.

AUTUMN

Starting to rain—
colorful umbrellas—
listen!—are singing!

From branch–hop!–
to branch–hop! Such a hurry!–
busy chipmunks.

A stroll for two
on the blooming duhlia—
happy snails.

Soaked, too,
dripping colors—
a rainbow.

Maybe next year
we'll travel together,
wild geese!

WINTER

Northern wind—
puppy growling
at the waves.

First snowflakes—
they fall softly, they melt,
they fall softly . . .

Even your ears,
covered with snow,
little donkey!

Dolls sleeping
under our tree—
Christmas Day.

In the rock's crack,
deep green, full of light—
winter blossom.